Dear Parents:

Congratulations! Your child is taking the first steps on an exciting journey. The destination? Independent reading!

STEP INTO READING® will help your child get there. The program offers five steps to reading success. Each step includes fun stories and colorful art or photographs. In addition to original fiction and books with favorite characters, there are Step into Reading Non-Fiction Readers, Phonics Readers and Boxed Sets, Sticker Readers, and Comic Readers—a complete literacy program with something to interest every child.

Learning to Read, Step by Step!

Ready to Read   Preschool–Kindergarten
• big type and easy words • rhyme and rhythm • picture clues
For children who know the alphabet and are eager to begin reading.

Reading with Help   Preschool–Grade 1
• basic vocabulary • short sentences • simple stories
For children who recognize familiar words and sound out new words with help.

Reading on Your Own   Grades 1–3
• engaging characters • easy-to-follow plots • popular topics
For children who are ready to read on their own.

Reading Paragraphs   Grades 2–3
• challenging vocabulary • short paragraphs • exciting stories
For newly independent readers who read simple sentences with confidence.

Ready for Chapters   Grades 2–4
• chapters • longer paragraphs • full-color art
For children who want to take the plunge into chapter books but still like colorful pictures.

STEP INTO READING® is designed to give every child a successful reading experience. The grade levels are only guides; children will progress through the steps at their own speed, developing confidence in their reading. The F&P Text Level on the back cover serves as another tool to help you choose the right book for your child.

Remember, a lifetime love of reading starts with a single step!

For Gail

Visit us on the Web!
StepIntoReading.com
rhcbooks.com

Educators and librarians, for a variety of teaching tools, visit us at
RHTeachersLibrarians.com

Library of Congress Cataloging-in-Publication Data
Names: Bramsen, Carin, author, illustrator.
Title: Duck & Cat's rainy day / by Carin Bramsen.
Other titles: Duck and Cat's rainy day
Description: New York : Random House, [2020]
Summary: Best friends Duck and Cat have very different reactions when it rains,
but Duck helps Cat find the fun.
Identifiers: LCCN 2019016392 | ISBN 978-1-5247-7171-3 (trade pbk.) | ISBN 978-1-5247-7172-0
(hardcover library binding) | ISBN 978-1-5247-7173-7 (ebook)
Subjects: | CYAC: Stories in rhyme. | Best friends—Fiction. | Friendship—Fiction. |
Rain and rainfall—Fiction. | Ducks—Fiction. | Cats—Fiction.
Classification: LCC PZ8.3.B7324 Duc 2019 | DDC [E]—dc23

Printed in the United States of America
10 9 8 7 6 5 4

This book has been officially leveled by using the F&P Text Level Gradient™ Leveling System.

Duck & Cat's
Rainy Day

by Carin Bramsen

Random House 🏠 New York

Split splat!

Duck and Cat.

Rain falls on Duck.

Yippee!
What luck!

Rain falls on Cat.

Oh, drat!
Not that!

Duck says,
"Let's play!"

Cat says,

"No way!"

Drip drop.

When will it stop?

Cat wears a frown.

Her head hangs down.

Duck climbs on Cat.

Look at that.

He will try
to keep Cat dry.

All set?

Not yet.

Cat's back is wet.

They both look back.

What is that?

Quack!

Quack!

While it stormed,
a puddle formed.

They take a look.

They see a cat.

She wears a hat.

A quacking hat!

A fluffy hat.

A wiggling hat.

A giggling cat.

Cat does not frown.

She wears a crown.

A funny crown.

A sunny crown.

The sky soon clears.

The sun appears.

These friends have fun
in rain or sun.